DARKEST NIGHTS

DARKEST NIGHTS
Copyright © 2022 by Kalen Jones

Published in the United States of America
ISBN   Paperback: 978-1-959165-09-5
ISBN   Hardback: 978-1-959165-29-3
ISBN   eBook: 978-1-959165-10-1

All rights reserved. No part of this publication may be reproduced, stored in a retrieval system or transmitted in any way by any means, electronic, mechanical, photocopy, recording or otherwise without the prior permission of the author except as provided by USA copyright law.

The opinions expressed by the author are not necessarily those of ReadersMagnet, LLC.

ReadersMagnet, LLC
10620 Treena Street, Suite 230 | San Diego, California, 92131 USA
1.619. 354. 2643 | www.readersmagnet.com

Book design copyright © 2022 by ReadersMagnet, LLC. All rights reserved.

Cover design by Ericka Obando
Interior design by Daniel Lopez

DARKEST NIGHTS

Kalen Jones

ReadersMagnet, LLC

PROLOGUE

I awake in complete darkness, which is unusual because I sleep with my night light on. As my eyes adjust, I realize I'm not in my room at all but my brother James's. I can make out his silhouette lying beside me on the ground. He must have carried me into his room, I think to myself, but why? I call out his name,

"James."

"Shh," he says sternly in a whisper. I lay quietly and exceptionally still, scared but not so sure why. Then I begin to hear a faint odd whimpering coming from the hall.

"Mom?" I say, just barely audible before I lift myself to run to her room but am caught by the wrist by James's firm grasp. He whispers,

"Whatever happens, don't scream and don't move; I'm serious; do not make a sound."

I nod as we lay side by side; the whimpering sound gets closer and closer to us until it seems to be right outside the door.

I can feel James's body start to shake, and it hits me; my big brother is afraid. I didn't think my brave older brother was scared of anything, so now I'm shaking. He hugs me hard as the door to his room bust open as if it was kicked in. I brave a peek, and a woman is standing stiff in the doorway. Even with the light pouring in, she seems featureless, almost as if she's a shadow. We don't move, even though with the door wide open, we are visible to whoever she is. James looks at me with tears in his eyes and says,

"I love you."

As soon as the words leave his lips, he is snatched through the air, and the door slams shut. I want to scream, to cry out for someone, anyone. But my brother's words ring in my ears. I promised. I hear the lady whimpering again until the sound is drowned out by the sirens. They grow louder and louder, and eventually, it seems they are on top of me. Once again, I feel the urge to yell for help, but I don't. The bedroom door burst open again, and this time I couldn't help it. A scream escapes my mouth. To my surprise, a man in uniform is at the door calling for backup on his radio. "John, we have a survivor."

What does he mean? A survivor? Survivor or what exactly, and just one? Suddenly the room is blurry, and I start to panic, "mom! James! Mom! James! "then everything goes black.

CHAPTER 1

"I hear the cry, that same odd whimpering. I am back in my brother's old room; it's dark but so familiar I can make out some of his things. I can see his trophies on the shelf, posters on the walls, and an old high school basketball jersey from when they won the championship. I am standing next to a boy that seems frozen in time. He is sitting so still when the door flies open, a woman looks at me with cold dark eyes, and immediately I glance down at the boy, and he stares at me. Like he is waiting for me to do something. Before I can even react, she points right at me, and that's when my fiance is usually shaking me awake."I tell my shrink.

He looks down, avoiding my face, it seems, and writes something in his book that is angled just out of my eyesight. I have been seeing a psychologist since I was eight. With my mom and brother dead, I had to stay with my aunt Tracie. I never knew my dad, but mom always said he died a hero. She didn't talk about him much, and when she did, tears would gloss over her eyes, so I never pushed the subject. Growing up, I didn't see much of my mom's sister, some kind of falling out. Just another one of those topics I learned to steer clear of. I couldn't complain, though. Despite having any children of her own, Aunt T was a great mom. No kids wasn't a choice, she had tried, but she couldn't get pregnant. Which eventually ended her marriage,

"15 years down the drain," she would always say.

"Uh umm... Kalen, are you still with me?" Dr. Harris says, snapping me back to reality from my trip down memory lane.

"Yes, sorry,"

I manage, fidgeting in my overly large chair. "About that dream, do you have it often?" He says, pen at the ready,

"More recently, I have had it about once a week, opposed to the twice a month I've gotten used to."

He's writing again, and I can't see. It is so frustrating. You would think I'd be used to it by now, but I always feel like I am being judged.

"And is the dream always the same? All of it?"

"only one thing changes, me as I grow in real life, I grow in the dream."

He goes silent, staring, almost lost in thought for a couple of seconds. I begin to regret my admission; what could that mean? Am I not growing out of something I should? My heart begins to race.

"Alright, that's all for today, Kalen. I will see you next week... Wednesday."

"Alright, doctor, thank you."

We shake hands and part ways.

"How was it?"

My fiance Kabrea asks as I am walking out of the door. She waits for me in the lobby every session, I tell her it isn't necessary, but she insists. She wants to be there with me, and it is comforting.

"It went well, and I still can't believe you made me come."

"Your auntie says I have to make sure you keep showing up, and this guy is affordable."

"I can't argue with Aunt T, but I've been doing this same song and dance for 18 years. This is my 7th shrink."

"And you are still having that same dream, my love."

She got me there. One thing I've learned being raised by women is to not argue because you will lose ten times out of ten. Kabrea grabs hold of my hand and stops walking. She looks me in the eyes, face very serious, and says,

"Did you tell him?"

"Of course I did; it's what I'm here for, right?"

I answer jokingly. Her glare becomes intense; I can tell I overdid it by laughing it off. She isn't playing.

"Did you tell him you are seeing her, you know, not just in your dreams?" her annoyance turns to worry, and I start to feel bad for joking about this at all.

"I don't think I'm ready yet."

I admit sadly. I can see her concern written all over her face, but she respects and accepts my answer.

"Just promise me you'll tell Dr. Harris soon, Kalen." she pleads.

"I promise, babe," I say sincerely,

but in the back of my mind, I don't know if I am ready to confront that truth. Saying it out loud makes it too real. That woman is the reason my mother and brother are dead, The reason I was bullied from kindergarten until graduation. Kids heard stories about what happened, and most of them assumed I killed my family. They called me crazy, a killer, an orphan; they even made up mean songs to sing. The pranks they would pull grew worse and worse every year. Thinking back on it, I feel my jaw clench and my body tense up, and Kabrea must have noticed too because she squeezed my hand a little tighter, but she didn't say a word. We rode in silence on the way home. The drive is only about 30 minutes, there and back, so not too long. As we pull up to our apartment, we see Aunt T's car in the driveway. No surprise there; she is very protective and continuously checks in after sessions. I never realized how much she looked like my mom, Keeshann. Long black hair that is always put up in some kind of intricate design, she always complains about how heavy it is, and I can only imagine. Her dark skin makes her beautiful hazel eyes stand out, which makes it almost impossible for her to hide her emotions even when she tries. Aunt T is about average height, and I outgrew her years ago, so as I was growing up, she'd always say,

"You might be bigger, but I'll still take you out."

That always made me chuckle, but I believe her, the athletic build from her sports and dance days, still presents itself. Before we can even step out of the car, Auntie asks, "how'd it go?" all enthusiastically.

"It was... Eye-opening," I say, overly exaggerated.

Both Aunt T and Kabrea roll their eyes and let out a small laugh.

"It was good," I say

Then Kabrea chimed in quickly,

"but he still hasn't told him yet."

as she looks at me with all the seriousness she can muster.

"WHAT?!"

I can practically see the steam billowing out of her ears as she glares at me. I am outnumbered here, so I choose my next words carefully.

"I'm just not ready yet,"

I get cut off abruptly, and I am honestly scared for what comes next, but Aunt T just hugs me tightly and says kind of aggressively. "Whenever you are ready, Kalen, but he needs to know. You understand me?"

"Yes, ma'am," I reply shakily, half because she intimidates me and half because I am not quite sure if I will ever actually be ready to share that with anyone else. Auntie and Kabrea share a nod and exchange a smile. They seem to be on the same page a lot; lately, I almost feel left out, it's like they have a secret I don't know, and it's driving me crazy, like an itch that I can't scratch. I know I can't coax anything out of these two. Every time I work up the nerve to ask what they are up to, the only response I get is an eye roll and giggles. Just like me to fall in love with women as stubborn as my Auntie. Kabrea and I met while at work; she was a server, and I was a janitor. That was five years ago, and now we have been engaged for about five years. I guess you could say we hit it off, you know, love at first sight and all that. Aunt Tracie was skeptical at first, like any mother, I suppose. She's always been extremely protective of me, and my love life has been no exception. After meeting her, though, she took an instant liking to her. I believe it has something to do with how alike they are, despite how different they are. She loves her now just as much as I do, and sometimes I think she might love her more than she does me.

"Tracie, you are more than welcome to stay for dinner" Kabrea's voice breaks my train of thought;

I'm out of my head and back in front of our apartment. Wonderful, I think to myself. They aren't finished with me yet.

"we're having tacos," she says with enthusiasm, almost trying to convince her.

"Thank you, my dear, but I've got to get going, actually. I just wanted to check on my baby."

I manage a little chuckle and an eye roll as we give hugs and wave goodbyes. I just dodged a bullet on therapy days; these ladies usually get going and don't stop. As she opens her car door, she hollers out,

"I am just a phone call away, honey, don't either of you ever hesitate. Love you guys."

"love you too!" We reply simultaneously.

I turn to walk into our apartment, and I am stopped in my tracks because the door is ajar. I see Kabrea still waving off Aunt T, and I decide to ignore it. The last thing I want to do is worry them. Plus, auntie was here when we pulled up; it's very possible she went inside to use the bathroom or get a glass of water. It's 90 degrees out here today. I reach for the handle before she turns around, so she doesn't notice it's opened, and I flinch. The doorknob is ice cold; it's not likely, especially in this heat.

"What's wrong, babe?" Her voice is soothing and warm.

I turn to see her face, and it's not there. I scream and stumble back into the open door. It's not my fiance in front of me, but that woman. Featureless except those intensely dark, cold eyes that seem to Pierce, my soul. She reaches for me. I try to back away and fall to the ground. That's when I hear her whimpering. My apartment is pitch black the only light spilling in from outside is shining directly on me. I close my eyes so tight it hurts.

"She's not real; she's not real,"

I repeat the mantra to myself over and over. The more I say it, though, the less I seem to believe it. Suddenly the room grows cold, just like the doorknob outside; I begin to shiver. The whimpering stops as a harsh voice utters "you, you, you're...." then booming and clear as day

"YOUR MINE!"

I throw my eyes open to see Kabrea's beautiful face staring back at me. We are standing on the front porch. I grab her face, grasping for reality because now I'm not sure what is real and what isn't. She jumps back, grabbing my hands.

"you're freezing babe, are you feeling okay?" seeing her concern and terror on her face I know I have to tell her what just happened. She'll never just let this go.

"She... She was here, right here" I stammered.

My voice is not nearly as strong as I'd like it to be, but I can't do this alone, and I know it. "She was right here, and this time, she spoke to me."

Chills run through me as I admit it. She looks at me horrified and asks

"What? What did she say?" her voice is shaking now?

"Your mine" my voice again weak and hoarse, mind reeling, replaying what I just saw. She must see it all over my face, she doesn't ask anything else, she just leaned in and planted a kiss on my lips and whispers

"I love you" as she slowly pulls away.

"I love you too."

I manage as I bravely open the door to our place. Sunlight beams from every window and cracked door. I take a deep breath, thank God for Kabrea's love for natural lighting.

CHAPTER 2

We cook dinner together, but not another word is said about the women. Me and Kabrea are both picky eaters, so there are no BBQ ribs, mashed potatoes, corn, and greens this way. Tacos, chicken and cheese quesadillas, frozen pizzas, that's as fancy as we get. Quick and easy, simple just like us. We dance around the kitchen while the Bluetooth speaker plays 90s R&B, singing at the top of our lungs and laughing at just how bad she is at it. The old neighbor lady must not mind, I'm sure she can hear but she never complains. These are the moments that give me the most joy when there's nothing but Kabrea and me against the world, all of my worries gone for the time being. We sit on the couch eating and telling recaps of our day. She tells me all about the book she is reading. I love hearing her talk about her readings. She speaks with so much passion and energy you'd think she was experiencing it all herself. She always talks with her hands, laughing when she recalls something funny and tears brim her eyes when something is sad. It's quite beautiful. After that, I give her a short version of my workday. I work in a factory so no lions, tigers, or…Wolves, but it gets interesting from time to time. After this, we sit in silence for a minute before she breaks it "you need to.."

I cut her short, already knowing where she's going.

"I'll tell Dr. Harris next week,"

I say looking at the ground, breaking our gaze. Slowly I lift my head and she's looking at me with her gorgeous green eyes and a half-smile on her lips

"thank you,"

she breathes. I feel some of the tension leave her body as I pull her close and squeeze her right.

"Anything for you my love"

I mumble into her sweet-smelling hair taking in this bit of normalcy. Felt safe, and home with her in my arms.

CHAPTER 3

"Shit!" I yelp as I jump realizing I have forgotten to set my alarm for work. I fumble around in the dark for my phone, I don't turn on the light because I don't want to wake Kabrea. Though I probably already have, she's quite the light sleeper. I squint at the phone as my eyes adjust to the light, the time reads 4:00 am, good. It's still early, I have to work at six and we only live around the corner. I'd like to go back to sleep but my heart is still racing from jumping up. As I lay in bed thoughts drift to my mother and the stories Aunt T used to tell about her. She was a beautiful woman, with a beautiful soul to match. She loved music and dancing. I vaguely remember her dancing around the kitchen when I was young. Making breakfast for me and James before school, singing the oldies to us as loud as she could manage. This brings a smile to my face, mom always loved helping people. If there was a person in need, she was always near. She volunteered at church every chance she got, Auntie says she was like that even as a child. We attended church for a while after she was gone. I always felt close to her there even though she was gone. I remember one time during service as I sat in the pew I felt a presence. Someone was next to me, not sitting there physically, but almost hovering over me. I was sure it was her. Once the pastor finished I told auntie how I thought mom was watching over us. How I felt her there with me.

"She was here Auntie, you always say she'll always be in my heart, but today I felt her, she was here!" I exclaimed, beaming with joy.

She looked at me like she had seen a ghost and said quietly,

"ok, baby, but let's keep this between us, our little secret, okay?" she tucked me under her arm as we made our way rather quickly to the front doors of the church. For the first time, that memory seems odd to me, and just before I get caught up in that, my alarm goes off.

"Ugh, I'm awake!" speaking to my cell phone as if it's going to talk back. On the plus side, it's Thursday technically my Friday so I don't waste any time getting going. I work Monday through Thursday, 10-hour shifts I'm eager to get this day over with and enjoy my weekend. I kiss Kabrea gently on the forehead

"I love you." she grunts, half-asleep,

"Have a good day."

"I love you too and I'll surely try my love," I whisper as I smile and cover her up. Work isn't my favorite place to be, not too fun or exciting. I work in a warehouse, a sorter department specifically. It's just a step up from the assembly line, I tried that, and standing in one place for ten hours a day just isn't for me. My body has got to be moving or I am liable to fall asleep. They play music over the loudspeaker and it's a decent mixture of genres, so if I forget my earbuds it's not a total bust. I love music and singing, it helps pass the time here. Nothing beats break time though and I don't mean lunch breaks when loads of people pile in one room and attempt to talk over each other, and fight for first in line to utilize a microwave. I'm talking about my break time, shut in a locked bathroom stall, and off my feet for a few minutes. I typically kill about 5 minutes here but it's Thursday so I may stretch that a tad longer, it's been a long week. The music from the floor plays in the restroom as well, which stinks but I can almost tune it out. Till the music changes from rock n roll to '90s R&B, catching my attention because me and Kabrea just reminisced about this song in the car this past weekend. That brings a smile to my face, thinking about her usually does. All of a sudden the song switches again and I'm snapped out of my little flashback. It's a really old song playing now, I recognize it but it takes me a second to place it. Then it hits me, my mom used to sing this song, I listen closely, I don't remember things about her often so I want to savor this when again the song suddenly changes. Something weird is going on, no song is playing longer than 30 seconds but each one means something to me. It's like they have been handpicked for me.

"beware of the creepy kid" echoes through the bathroom and my blood runs cold. I'm frozen in place, I can't believe my ears.

"Who killed his mom and brother, you better run, you better hide, better duck for cover!"

How is this even possible? Is this some kind of joke? It's on the radio! My mind is racing, who could be playing this? Why? I will myself to stand and pull my pants up shaking. I fumble with my belt for longer than I'd like. Forced to listen to the nursery rhyme that blamed me for the death of my family., the one that ruined my social life for years.

"If he catches you, you'd better scream and shout! But by then you may be through so watch out, watch out, WATCH OUT, Kalen's coming for you!" the song clicks off and so do the lights. It takes a couple of seconds that feel like hours for me to gain control of my hand and unlock the stall. All the while waving my other hand hoping to catch the motion sensor for the lights. My heart is racing and sweat is dripping from my face. Finally, the stall door swings open and I am not at work at all. I'm standing inside my old elementary school. The giant welcome to Montgomery Elementary, where our students rise to success! A banner hanging right above my head. The halls are dark and cold. I see a light from one of the classrooms in the distance so I head towards it. Once I reach the door and I am about to open it when I look through the window and see myself! My younger self, in Mrs.King's class, I am silently crying while being hit with spitballs repeatedly. I am about to burst through the door then the entire scene vanishes before my eyes. I look away hurt and confused when I see another classroom light up just down the hall. I sprint to the door and I see Mr. Hines with his back to the class writing an assignment on the board while the kids pass around a note and giggle. One of them throws it at the back of my head I open it up "MURDERER" tears fill my eyes and I get up to leave. Mr. Hines yells after me and the kids begin to chant that awful nursery rhyme they made up. My younger self bursts through the door and runs right past me until he disappears into the darkness in front of Mrs. Kirk's old room. The light comes on and there little me is, eating lunch alone. Mrs. Kirk was the only person in that school who seemed to care. She saw and heard the other kids bully me. They would throw my lunch away and call me names. Mrs. Kirk offered to let me eat my lunch in peace in her classroom. As I watched myself sit lonely and silent tears fell from my eyes. The memories flooded my mind; they hurt more than I even remembered. Another light comes on down the hall and I'm not sure I can handle seeing anymore but it's at the end of the hall so I walk down praying I will soon wake up from whatever hell I am in. I make it to the room and peer in ready to face whatever awful scene is next and am slightly confused. It's not one of my classes at all. Every kid in there is staring at this girl who is standing up in her chair and seems to be yelling but I can't hear a thing even though the door is open. Then I notice something looming behind her, it's very familiar. I take a step closer to the doorway trying to get a better look, the screaming girl looks directly at me, eyes piercing my soul, and the door slams shut. I sit frozen at the door, that girl, I've seen her before but I can't remember where. The room goes dark and the exit sign has illuminated ahead. I am more than ready to get out of here. I push open the door and find myself out on the playground where I see a little boy curled up in a ball on the ground while three little girls skip circles around him singing "beware of the creepy kid"

I look around in shock, that song is about me, and this kid is not me at all, maybe a small resemblance but definitely not the younger me, and this isn't a memory of mine. Before I have much time to contemplate this the girl's voices begin to come out in a demonic growl and the woman emerges behind them from the darkness. She points in my direction and the girls stop and stare directly at me as the boy crawls to me grabbing my leg tightly. The woman growl's "you're mine; I'm coming."

The little girls started to call my name first softly; then it grew deeper and deeper, louder and louder. I closed my eyes telling myself this isn't real, I opened them back up and my supervisor, Brad, was looking at me with concern.

"Kalen," Brad says as I glance around and I am on the production floor. A shiver runs through me

"weren't you going to the restroom? Are you feeling alright, you look like you've seen a ghost?" scrambling for words to say I am lost but I manage

"I was uhm waiting…"

I'm trying to get my head around what just happened to me. I never made it to the restroom because my work had started to pile up in front of me but whatever that was, felt so real it scares me. Brad just looks at me puzzled for a moment and says "alright, well okay" and moves on. He is a good boss but a little off sometimes now I'm worried he is looking at me the way I and my coworkers look at him. Going to the bathroom is very unlikely now, just thinking about it makes my heart race. I finish out my shift without so much as a glance in that direction. Off and I can't wait to call Kabrea. I need to tell her what happened. I know she is going to want me to tell Aunt T and Dr. Harris and I'm prepared. Auntie just might freak but she likes to be kept in the loop and I owe her that, besides if I don't clue her in I know Kabrea will. I clock out and race to the car, using my Bluetooth to call Kabrea. It barely rings once before she picks it up, I always call on my way home from work so she anticipates my call.

"Hey there my love," she answers with such life in her voice.

I want to change my mind about telling her I'd hate to ruin her mood or scare her while she's home alone. That's out of the question. That moment's pause was all she needed.

"What is it, babe?"

Sometimes I hate how much this woman knows me. The life in her voice turns to fear. I take a deep breath and let it all out. I tell her everything and tears sting my eyes as I try not to let them fall.

"She's coming for me, it's getting worse."

The line has grown quiet, and I break the silence admitting,

"I'm scared."

"don't be. We will take care of this, I promise we've got this, we'll get through it together."

She always knows what to say, she is my rock. Truly. She's trying to stay strong but I hear the sniffles she tries to hide. I can tell she wants to believe the words she just said but I can feel that she doesn't.

"Let's go see your Aunt when you get home."

Almost like she can read my mind.

"Good idea baby, I'll call and make sure she's home. I'll be there shortly, get ready. I love you."

I'm so focused on getting home I barely remember the drive from work. I pull up and Kabrea is standing in the doorway waiting for me as soon as I open my car door she's in my arms. She looks me in the eyes and slips her hand in mine and leads me into the house. I hop in the shower quickly so we don't get stuck in traffic.

CHAPTER 4

Aunt T lives in the city, on the outskirts, close enough that she can get groceries without driving 45 minutes and not feel safe if danger were to arise.

"I like my space, but I like my safety even more," she always said.

I think she secretly likes the nightlife and people watching but she'll never admit it. She insisted we buy a house and we stay close so she only lives 10 minutes away. I make it there in record time in my HHR, I drive it like a corvette though, and typically Kabrea complains but there are no objections today. We ride in silence holding tight to each other's hands. The tension, fear, and uncertainties hanging in the air threaten to suffocate us both. Auntie knew right away that something was off by the look on our faces.

"What is it, baby? What's wrong" she asks frantically as she ushers us into the living room. "What's wrong?" she almost yells with worry as she moves her things, making room for us on the couch. Neither of us has said a word and I can see the irritation creeping onto her face. Kabrea finally speaks up, soft and full of worry "it's getting worse; he saw her again."

We both stare at the ground, not wanting to see Aunt T's reaction, knowing I'm going to find disappointment.

"Kalen, why didn't you say anything?" as I raise my head to answer her, a picture on the table catches my eye. My jaw drops and both women follow my gaze. I stand up grabbing hold of the photo to make sure I'm not seeing things. It is a picture of Auntie as a young girl; I know because she hasn't changed a bit, but she's standing hand in hand with the little girl from earlier.

"Aunt T, who is this beside you?"

As I point shakingly at the picture in my hand.

"That's your mother," she says

She takes the picture from me and stares at it longingly before she gently puts it back exactly as I found it. I can tell it means a lot to her and tears glisten in her eyes and she looks back at me, seemingly searching for words. Before she can say anything else I say

"Auntie I saw her today. I saw that little girl."

the lights shut off abruptly. I look at Auntie and Kabrea for information, to ensure it isn't happening again. Kabrea jumps up and grabs my arm, keeping me close and confirming that they are experiencing this too. The temperature drops and it's so cold I can see my breath. We are all silent until I manage, "no one move, no one make a sound."

I've put on a brave face but I'm really falling apart, I can't believe this isn't just in my head. Then I hear the whimpering followed by footsteps. I feel Kabrea shaking next to me and I look to Aunt T about to reassure her but I notice she is sitting in her chair unbothered. I fear for us all as the woman moves into view, still featureless except those cold hollow eyes. Aunt T stands up firmly and angrily says

"YOU CAN'T HAVE HIM!"

The lights come back on, the room temperature rises and the woman she's gone. Confused and conflicted, Kabrea and I share a look and simultaneously turn to Aunt Tracie who is still standing, gazing in the direction the women came. Slowly she turns to us, fist clenched tight, eyes narrowed, ready for war it seems. She looks at me and Kabrea and whispers.

"You need to tell him now, we can't wait any longer."

Kabrea nods"there is something I need to tell the both of you," Auntie says

With a serious voice, Kabrea sits down, takes a deep breath, and almost lets herself relax, while I feel totally in the dark, looking back and forth between the two of them, waiting for an explanation. Kabrea pats the couch next to her for me to come sit as I do. She turns to me with tears spilling down her cheeks, I start to panic, having no idea what to expect. She smiles through her tears,

"WE ARE PREGNANT!"

I let out the breath I didn't even notice I was holding, and I beam with joy, tears once again forming in my eyes,

"I'm going to be a dad." I exclaim

I embrace her, holding Kabrea and our unborn child as close as any two bodies can get.

"I love you" I whisper into her ear.

"I love you Kalen."

she sobs into my chest.

"I wanted to make it special, this isn't how I wanted to tell you. I am so sorry."

I chuckle, it's just like her to be concerned with little things like that.

"Babe, it's okay. This is perfect."

I kiss her forehead as I let go and look back at Aunt T. She is sitting emotionless, and eerily still.

"Auntie, what is it?" I ask

My joy from the news is slowly turning to fear. She looks at me with an expression that says,

"I am sorry."

before beginning her story.

"Your grandfather he… He loved your grandmother so much, she was his whole world. They were inseparable and their relationship seemed like something straight from a fairy tale. Until one night there was screaming and yelling coming from their bedroom. They were arguing before I could even decipher what it was about. I noticed smoke and that smoke turned to flames. My dad burst into our bedroom almost hitting me with the door. He grabbed me and your momma and raced to the front door. Flames surrounded the door but dad gripped us tight and slammed his body against it with all his strength. We landed on the front lawn confused and panicked me and Keeshann jumped up and frantically searched for mom. Dad had gotten us out but there was so sign of her anywhere. As I was about to ask about her I saw her standing in the doorway… Burning but still alive. We could hear her crying out in pain. Your grandfather hollered at us to look away trying his best to shield us from the horrific scene before us. We of course did as we were told but the damage was done. Her screams and her scorched body would forever be burned into my mind. I was only six and your mama was eight, daddy never talked about that night but he cried almost every day after it. He was never the same man again. Broken, distant, and eventually even scary. I caught him in his study often reading books, not like the Great Gastby or Huck Finn. Strange things like a book of black magic and witchcraft, the secrets of voodoo. He kept a picture of mom's charred remains on his desk, it was truly disturbing. All you could see was her eyes. I don't think he ever meant for us to see it but we became pretty curious to find out why he was being so secretive truthfully we just wanted our dad back. It felt like we lost both our parents in that fire. We had been staying in an apartment while the house was being rebuilt and me and your mom longed to get back to our home. We thought maybe being there we would get our father back, we were young and a tad bit naive. Things become worse, much worse. He stayed up well into the night, he would scream, slam doors, we'd hear things breaking throughout the house. I climbed into bed with your mom on many nights too afraid to sleep alone. He talked to himself, the walls, someone who just wasn't there. Almost like he was taking orders from someone in his head. We worried about him losing his mind. There were days he didn't remember who we were, who he was. After about two years it all just stopped. He was far from the dad we knew and loved but he almost completely snapped out of whatever he was going through and he played his part as our father. He was around more, playing games with us, best of all no more screaming and slamming doors in the middle of the night. It was peaceful compared to recent times. It didn't last long, every night Keeshann would tell me goodnight, it was normal but then one night she turned over to say

"Goodnight, mom"

I smiled ear to ear. It sort of gave me this calming feeling, I knew everyone coped in their way and hers was much easier to deal with than dads. Believing mom was with us in some way brought me happiness I had missed. Then, on her 10th birthday, things got intense. I never mentioned her nightly ritual to dad. In hindsight, I probably should have but I didn't want to upset him, and some nights I could swear I'd hear mom crying faintly, it would keep me up late sometimes. But when we were celebrating your mama, she was just about to blow out the candles and she smiled that million-dollar smile. She looked at me and daddy and said

"I don't even need this wish, my only one has come true; mom is here with us."

The candles blew out viciously along with all the lights in the house. I heard the same faint crying that kept me up and a shiver ran down my spine. I looked to your grandfather as the lights began to flicker back on, and he was standing up, his dark skin now pale and the smile gone from his face. He looked around the room in complete shock then hurried to his room without a word and didn't return for the night. I started to believe maybe, my dad had done something with all of those books he was obsessed with before."

"Aunt T" I interrupted just then,

my mind reeling, I had so many thoughts, so many questions but one I needed to ask. "Auntie, do you think my mom did the same thing grandpa Charles did? Am I seeing grandma?"

I instantly regretted saying that last part. Aunt T stood but fiercely

"THAT THING IS NOT YOUR GRANDMOTHER THAT IS NOT MY MOM!" She yells tears glisten once again in her eyes as she fights the urge to cry. I sat back joining Kabrea once more on the couch and waited for T to finish the story, eager to have all the information. Auntie slowed her erratic breathing, inhaling deeply and settling back into her seat before continuing.

"Every night after that day, we heard the same whimpering you have. It would stop right outside our bedroom door, making my blood run cold and sending chills through my body. Keeshann though, it was like she didn't hear it at all she sat unbothered. She would talk to the women often, about her boyfriend, school bullies, and just like dad there was never anyone there. It went on for years and eventually I got used to it accepting that this is our reality. Then your mamma met James, he was a troubled young man but your mom set him straight. She loved him so much she stopped talking to the women and asked me not to ever speak about it. She didn't want him to think she was crazy. She would say"

I began to get more intrigued. I had never heard anything about my father. After all these years this is the first time anyone has ever mentioned him to me. I didn't even know his name, so my brother is James Jr. It's refreshing to know they shared something so simple as a name. James was an amazing older brother, the only true father figure in my life.

"Kalen pay attention" Auntie yells,

snapping me back from my daydream. She knows me too well and she continues her story.

"That is when the spirit that we believed was our mother got angry. The whimpering sound came every night but her actions became increasingly violent now when she stopped at our door she would bang on the door loudly for what felt like forever. Keeshann would wake screaming in the night with deep scratches on her legs, many nights I'd try to stay awake to protect her. She was so afraid she hardly slept anymore but it was no use. The woman pulled at her legs trying to yank her off the bed." Auntie paused,

whipping tears from her eyes, goosebumps freckled my skin and Kabrea sat motionless with her eyes wide.

"The worst part was when we finally told dad; he didn't say anything; he retreated to his room just like on Keeshanns birthday for hours. Sometimes we wouldn't see him for days except when coming and going to work."

I feel Kabrea grab my thigh, and I hold her closer feeling the anxiety pulsing through our bodies. I can tell she wants to speak, probably has a million questions but she stays silent for now listening intently. "Eventually, we got so worried we spied on our dad; we knew we shouldn't, but we needed answers. So, we stood outside his door some nights straining to hear anything. He'd say take me, take me instead just leave my girls alone, please, as he sobbed. For a while, we thought he was praying and we're glad to know he was listening to us. We believed it worked when he was done the women would stop for a day, a week, and sometimes even longer. When I was sixteen your mom announced that she and James got engaged and your big brother was on the way."

I saw a smile creep across her face like she was reliving a happy memory.

CHAPTER 5

"Things were normal; they were great! For the first time in ten years, we were happy with new life coming into the world. It was beautiful. Well, just like you, Kalen, Keeshann started seeing the lady again in her dreams."

The smile that lay on her face shrinks as the pain in her eyes grows.

"At first, I didn't believe her. I thought she just wanted attention, I was in denial the lady had been gone for months, why would she come back now? What could she possibly want? I just didn't understand. I made excuses in my head. I wasn't convinced until one night we were all sitting at the dining room table talking after dinner. Suddenly the room grew still; it was almost like life had been sucked from the place and time seemed to stop, the lights flickered and burst, and the entire room was ice cold. I made eye contact with Keeshann and we both knew exactly what was happening" Kabrea's grasp grew tighter. I can tell she wants the story to end but needs to know what happens.

"She was back, first the whimpering sound then it was like the darkness brought her to life right in front of our eyes. She pointed straight at your mom. My, my, MINE! In a growl that would make anyone shiver"

I am freaking out. My heart is racing. It is a lot to take in, I knew none of this about my family, and now my wife and child are in danger because of me I can feel sweat beading on my forehead.

"At that moment, our dad jumped in front of us, demanding that she take him instead. He begged her to please leave his girls alone, and said he would go in our place."

I couldn't keep quiet any longer, my nerves were going crazy. So many questions "did it work? Did she accept the offer? Why?"

Auntie looked at me with such sadness in her eyes it brought tears to mine.

"Patience, child, I'm getting there. The lady now sizing dad up lets out a hideous growl that shook the house, approaching my dad. Circling him, examining him, contemplating his offer. Dad was lifted into the air like a puppet on strings and brought face to face with the women. He looked back at me and Keeshann and said I love you both very much, let that baby know I... Before he was able to finish the women's fingers pierced his chest pulling out his heart. She looked at us heart in hand as if mocking us then she disappeared as quick as she came letting Dad's lifeless body drop to the floor with a thud that still echoes in my head."

The room is completely still, everyone is crying, frozen, not able to speak. Auntie dries her eyes and continues

"We both rushed to Dad's side, sobbing uncontrollably. Your mom yelled for me to call 911. Dad was dead, your mom and I were in shock, we were all taken to the hospital, and there we got to hear your big brother's heartbeat for the first time. At that moment my heart swelled, the silver lining to the tragedy we just endured but your mother's mind was elsewhere."

Suddenly Kabrea gasped, looking straight into my eyes, her face pale, her body visibly shaking. She lets go of my hand and protectively grabs her belly. Tears form in her eyes as the words fall from her mouth, it sounds like I'm underwater. In my mind, I know she's right but I don't want to believe it.

"She wants our baby!"

"No that's not true right Auntie, grandpa ended this bullshit right?" I yell frantically; the air around me grows thick, and a nauseating feeling comes over me. Kabrea and I stare at Aunt T intently waiting for an answer. She moves closer and grabs our hands and squeezes them

"He did, or so we thought but after your father died saving you all from another fire"

I cut her off,

"Wait, What?! Another fire? Where? How?"

I can feel something like anger building up inside me. How have I lived so long and known nothing of my own family?

She held up her hand, stopping my manic rant, looking at me with sad eyes like she can feel my pain radiating from me.

"At the same house, our old one. The one you, me, and your momma grew up in."

"But how, what are the odds? What could be causing these fires? How is this even related?"

My voice is shaking now just like my hands. I am bursting with questions and I feel like we don't have time for them all. I stare at the ground trying hard to gather my thoughts and make some sense of all this.

Auntie says softly,

"We don't know for sure, but I have my theories. This entity has been plaguing this family for generations. I tried to distance myself years ago when I walked away from your mother. Whatever she is, she feeds on destruction, loneliness, fear, and it is good at getting what it wants. We found the books in my father's study as young girls; I was curious. I would sneak in when I could and read. I wanted so badly to understand my daddy and why he was doing the strange things he did. We knew he was talking to someone, something, and I secretly wanted it to be my mom. We missed her so much it hurt, but after my little research all I could come up with was that dad had contacted something from the other side and that sent chills up my spine. Everything in those books warned against trying to contact a spirit, being cautious because it wasn't always who you thought. Desperation was a weakness when it came to that, demons and such could smell it and would without a doubt, feed on it. I didn't sneak in to read anymore, I was too scared. But, I would stay up and eavesdrop at daddy's door when I could, trying to hear something, anything. One night, I heard voices when we were supposed to be asleep, so I creeped over to his study and with my ear pressed to the door I heard her. She sounded like mom, but I felt it in my gut, it wasn't. Daddy believed it though, he missed her so much it didn't take much convincing. I heard him promise it something. I tried hard to tell myself I had heard wrong, that my daddy would never give us up."

"What do you mean give you up? He gave you up? That's why my mom is gone? Was it him? I almost scream these words at Aunt T, and I instantly feel bad. It's not her fault.

"But, if…if he gave himself up, why is mom gone? If this woman, this thing, just wants a soul, why is she not still here?"

Auntie takes a deep breath and begins again,

"Well, to be fair, I don't think this entity is very forthcoming, they are smart and know exactly what buttons to push to get people to do what they want. I did lots of reading back then on these things. I know now I heard correctly, my daddy agreed to sacrifice his first born child just to talk to his wife again. I don't think he knew what he was promising, I have to believe that he didn't understand what was asked of him at the time. Once he died though, and things returned to normal I thought we were done with it all. She wasn't showing up, Keeshann was doing great, and then it all just started over, like there was no curse on our family. The fire took your father, and Keesh was so distraught. I did all that I could to be there for her, but she missed James so much, it was like deja-vu. She was spiraling, falling down the same hole your grandpa did. She yearned for James day in and day out, she became obsessed with seeing him again. I caught her with many of the same books dad kept in his office and I knew where this was headed. I never told your momma what I overheard that night, maybe if I had she would still be here and this wouldn't be happening."

Kabrea spoke in a whisper, "You were just a kid, you can't blame yourself for the sins of your father."

"I just couldn't aid my only family left in destroying her life. She asked for my help and I refused. After seeing what all this darkness did to Dad I couldn't. I begged her to reconsider what she was doing, I told her I didn't trust this nonsense; I tried to reason with her."

Auntie was crying harder now, tears rolling down her cheeks as she struggled to say what came next. She explained how much regret she carried and how she never meant for it to end up like this. I heard it all but my head was swimming, I felt like I was dreaming, this was all too much.

Auntie cleared her throat and it brought me back,

"I told her to never speak to me again. I felt so betrayed in that moment that I didn't see her hurt, I yelled at her! Those were the very last words I spoke to my own sister."

She put her head in her hands and sobbed uncontrollably.

I moved closer to comfort her, wrapping my arm around her shoulders, maybe more for me than her I couldn't tell. I heard Aunt T mumble something but between all the crying I couldn't quite make it out. I got on my knees in front of her and told her how much I love her and grabbed her hands and she looked me in my eyes with so much sorrow that I felt it in my soul.

"She wants your first born, I think your momma made the same mistake my daddy did. She promised that woman something unknowingly. I know Keesh, she would never have let anyone take that baby. That thing created chaos, I think it started those fires to destroy lives and then feeds off the weakness of the loved ones. She gets them to say they'd do anything, give anything to see or hear from the ones they've lost. They just don't realize what they are going to give up until it's too late."

Kabrea moves closer to us now, and it's like she was reading my mind, "But if someone has always gone in place of these babies, and the debt it paid, why us? We haven't tried contacting anyone, what have we done to warrant this?"

Tears are pouring from her eyes but her voice doesn't waiver.

She is so strong, stronger than I ever knew. I am truly lucky. I can't even get words out because I'm in such awe of this beautiful woman in front of me. She has no idea how much I need her. I grab her hand and I can almost feel her strength flow into my body. I know that no matter what I will find a way to protect these two precious lives. I stand up,

"I love you Aunt T, we will stop this." My voice much more confident than I feel inside.

"I just think this thing is much stronger now and while an adult sacrifice is slowing her down I believe she plans to collect the two children she was promised. She took James Jr. from us, and now the next child in our line is…."

She looks down at Kabrea's belly.

"I love you both dearly, but I have read all the books, scoured the internet, talked to a priest, and come up with nothing, not a damn thing!"

"I will find a way, I have to."

I mutter as I squeeze both of their hands, giving them both the most sincere smile I can muster. Kabrea and Auntie both look up at me with eyes full of hope.

"We can stop her babe, we can. I just have to figure out how."

For a few minutes we all just sit there in silence and the tension in the room could be cut with a knife. Kabrea yawns and I know we should go, she needs to rest, this was all too much. Leaving Aunt T's is hard, but I check the clock, it's nine o'clock. We have been here for hours. Our emotions are running high and as hard as it might be, sleep is necessary. We say our goodbyes, give out hugs, and head to the car.

The ride home was full of tears, quiet ones. Kabrea talks first, her voice full of worry

"How can we stop this?"

All I can manage is

"I don't know."

It breaks my heart; I want to have all the answers; I want it to be over. We sit in silence the rest of the way home.

CHAPTER 6

Sleep evades me, I give Kabrea some tylenol for her headache and lay with her until she's fast asleep, then I head to the computer. Research. I need to find a way, I need to save my family. I read anything and everything I can find, by the time I am done I have concluded this entity has to be a demon, and a very powerful one at that, and if my family members really have promised it a child then stopping it will be next to impossible.

I shut off my phone thinking maybe I can get a couple hours sleep, but no luck. My mind is moving a million miles a minute, night turns to day as I lay there. I get up and feel myself just going through the motions of my morning routine. We both do our best to stay positive and not let this new found knowledge consume us.

I shared the little information I found last night with her over breakfast and it sent a shudder through her.

I sit and admire Kabrea's wavy brown hair and how her green eyes illuminate her face. She is a lot like Tracie, she doesn't hide her emotions very well with me. I can see the fear behind her eyes and the way she's keeping a hand protectively over her belly almost constantly. Me and that baby are blessed to have this woman in our lives. She is going to make the best mother, I think to myself as I stare.

CHAPTER 7

The days ahead are dark and I feel like we are awaiting impending doom. I haven't seen "the woman" for a couple days now, and I don't know how to feel about that. Tomorrow I meet with my psychiatrist and I am prepared to tell him everything, everything Aunt T told me about grandpa, my mom, the woman, all of it. I am afraid of what his reaction will be but I need to get this off my chest. I am scared he might think I am crazy, and lock me up, but I am more scared for my unborn child and I am at a loss.

I walk into the kitchen and Kabrea is on the phone, I walk up behind her and wrap my arms around her, placing my hands on her little baby bump.

"Yes, Friday is fine, yes, ma'am. We will see you Friday at three, can't wait."

She hangs up the phone and turns to face me. She just set up our ultrasound. She tries to look excited, and so do I but you can tell it's forced. I need to be strong for the both of us. I am usually a lot better at hiding my emotions but it is proving more difficult than normal.

"Dinner tonight, be ready, my love," I say

I wink at her, giving her my best flirty smile. I want to take her mind off of things even if only for an hour. I am going to keep the conversation light and about our upcoming wedding. We will talk about the colors, flowers, cake, and how her dress is coming along. I want the night to be filled with love and looking forward to the future.

This week has been one of the toughest, and the nights are long and dark. She has cried herself to sleep while I lay awake. Books and papers I have printed for research cover our night stand, I won't give up. I read a different book every night on demons, and contacting the dead, or how to get rid of evil, and the supernatural. I pray each day harder than the next, for just a sign, anything to help me save us all.

When I get off work, I race to the store to find flowers as beautiful as her. I pick her up from the house and greet her with a kiss as I open her door. She is wearing a gorgeous black dress and heels. Her make-up is done, and she is glowing.

"These are beautiful, babe, thank you!" She says,

smiling from ear to ear.

"Not as beautiful as you are."
We both must have had the same idea for today. We need some sense of normalcy in the midst of all this crazy.

First things first, we head to my appointment, time to pour out my heart and be gawked at like I'm some lunatic. I don't know if I am ready for that, but the ride there is filled with laughter and singing everything from country to rock to r&b of course. Kabrea would touch her belly from time to time and I could see the worry creep into her eyes, but I placed my hand over her not saying anything, just letting her know I am here.

CHAPTER 8

As we pull up to the office building I brace myself, today's session is going to be rough. Today I tell him everything, no holding back. I take a deep breath as we step out of the car.

Kabrea lays her hand on my chest, "You got this babe, I will be right outside if you need me." she says

with the gentlest voice. Then she kisses me and tells me she loves me.

"I love you too, thank you….for just being you Kabrea, I couldn't do this without you." I whisper in her ear.

Dr. Harris is in his chair as usual when I enter the room. Pen and notepad at the ready on his lap, his eyes meet mine as he raises a hand toward the couch inviting me to have a seat.

"Hello Kalen, how are you today?"

Feels like a loaded question, but I reply calmly "I'm doing alright doc."

"Looks like there is a lot on your mind, are you sleeping alright?"

I take one last deep exhale as I prepare myself to tell it all. I tell Dr. Harris everything, starting with my grandparents, explaining what Auntie told me about her and my parents. I tell him almost word for word what she told me and I realize that he isn't writing anything down, his notepad is actually sits on his desk and he is leaned forward elbows resting on his knees listening intently as the words flow out of my mouth. His expression is hard to read, I can't tell what is going through his mind. I don't know if he is truly interested in what I am saying or the fact that I am saying it at all. I've said more today than in all of our sessions combined and I am sure that is a shock.

I continue still searching his dark brown eyes, looking for some sort of sign, of what, I am not totally sure. That I'm not crazy maybe? I get to the part where the demon, woman, whatever "it" is and I can tell that stunned him. I don't think he saw that coming, but I didn't stop, I went on to tell him about how I have seen the woman in my dreams, and then in my house, at work.

"She's coming for my child" I say out of breath as my story comes to an end. I frantically look at the clock, afraid I have used up all my time and I won't get any advice from this session and it will all be a waste of time. The room grows still, my breaths come thundering in the quiet, the rooms only light the quickly fading sun. I'm having a panic attack.

Dr. Harris' voice breaks the silence,

"That was…. A Lot Kalen. It sounds like you have unfinished business."

I stare at him hard, waiting for some further explanation.

"I believe you and your Aunt have created this thing, this woman, in your minds to help cope with the loss of your loved ones."

It hits me hard, knocking the wind right from my lungs. He doesn't believe me, his words are insulting and cut deep even though they were said with such compassion, it also sounds like pity.

"Dr. Harris, this woman is REAL!" I blurt almost violently.

"Kalen, it's okay. It is very common to believe something unbelievable, especially when you are trying to make sense of something so traumatic. But you have to be able to admit that and work through it, let it go."

I stand up now, hot, ready to scream. "She is real." I insist.

"Alright, calm down, we are past schedule and I have another patient waiting. So, I'll send you with this, go to the house. I assume it is still abandoned." He looks at me quizzically. I nod in confirmation.

"Go there, find what you're looking for, get your closure. And we will talk more about this next week." He says

He stands to walk me to the door.

At this point, I am eager to leave; I can't get out of this confining space fast enough.

"Have a good day, Doc. And thank you, for everything."

Kabrea meets me with a huge hug as I step into the waiting room.

"What did he say?" she asks

As she releases me from her embrace.

"He thinks I'm insane, he believes me and Auntie have conjured this all up in our heads to deal with the grief. He says she can't be real." I say

gritting my teeth at relaying such a ludicrous accusation.

"But, that's impossible. I saw her too! At your Aunt's just last week, and I am on the outside of all the so-called grief!" she demands.

The memory floods my mind and I want to storm back in there and prove to him I am right. But, I restrained myself. He didn't believe me before one more person's encounter is only going to make him think we all need help.

"Did he say anything else or did he just insult you the whole time?" She asks, anger filling her voice.

"Yeah, he said that I should go to the house."

She stops dead in her tracks and looks at me with concern.

"If you go, I am going with you." She says sternly

I know right then there is no changing her mind. Kabrea is as strong willed as they come, once her mind is made up that's all there is to it.

"How do you know I even want to go?" I ask,

smiling at her because she just knows me so well, and to be known that way feels good, especially when I have been questioning if I even know myself these last few days.

"Because I know you Kalen, all the way to your core."

We allowed ourselves a good laugh that lasted the whole way home. Dinner was filled with wonderful conversation, not at all related to the insane events of recent. We talked about books, movies, baby names, we joked and just totally enjoyed ourselves. Something we haven't seemed to do at all the last week or two. As we clean up after dinner together I tell her that we can go to the house tomorrow, she nods and we continue to talk late into the night not wanting it to end. It was perfect.

Finally, we drift off to sleep, and all seems well.

CHAPTER 9

A loud noise startles me awake. BOOM. I hear a door slam, I slowly lift myself from my bed, only to realize that this isn't my bedroom at all. I turn frantically to wake Kabrea and she isn't there. BOOM. Another door slams. I climb mindlessly from the edge of the bed to the floor, and instantly recognize that I am somehow back in my brother's room all those years ago. Only this time there is a baby crib in the center of the room. Chills run down my spine as I move closer to the crib. With every step I take though I am moving further away from the baby bed, not closer.

Suddenly the room's temperature drops, and another loud BOOM comes from the hallway, and I hear a baby start to cry. I look towards the sound of the child and I see nothing but darkness, I turn back to the crib and it has vanished and Aunt T stands in its place.

"Auntie" I stammer

"Are you okay? What are you doing here?" I askin full on panic mode now.

"I love you, son." She manages

As she's ripped from the room, BOOM! The door slams loudly as she disappears.

I scream at the top of my lungs, gasping for air, as Kabrea pulls me from my nightmare.

"It's alright baby, it's okay. We are fine. You're fine."

She holds me close, like she has on countless nights before.

"You should call work, and tell them you can't make it in today, we need to finish this."

I know she's right, so I don't argue or point out that I still have no idea what to do. I call into work, they won't be happy, but my family has to come first. I need to go to the house, and I'd rather not go when the sun is going down, so during the day it will be best.

It's almost nine by the time we get out of bed, determined looks on our faces. We desperately want this to be over with, and it seems like confronting this thing might be our best and only option. I know God is on our side, and he will see us through this one way or another.

Kabrea's phone rings, and I look around for mine remembering I forgot to charge it through the night. Oh well.

"Who is it?" I ask.

"Tracie." She replies as she answers the phone.

And the look on her face tells it all; something is clearly wrong.

"What is it?" I say, scared to hear the answer. She doesn't respond, just stares for a moment,

"What is it? What's going on?" I ask again, a little impatient this time.

"Your Aunt, she….she's at the house. She sounded scared. Kalen, we have to hurry. She was whispering, I could hardly hear what she was saying but it almost sounded like a goodbye! What has she done?"

She gets up so fast and goes for her clothes and the keys before I can even process what she has just said. I race to get dressed, my heart is pounding and my breath is catching, I'm crying and I didn't even notice. I wipe the tears as we walk out the door.

I speed to the old house. When we get there it's hard not to think about how beautiful the property is. Even with all the overgrown weeds, fire damage and chipping paint the light blue color and huge front porch it is truly stunning.

Aunt T's car is in the driveway, and my stomach sinks. It's real, she's really here, that wasn't some trick. Auntie is truly in trouble. I turn to Kabrea,

"Promise me, you'll stay in the car."

"I can't just sit here Kalen, you might need me!" She argues.

"I need you to be safe Kabrea, please stay in the car until I come back. Don't risk your life or the precious baby's. If I want nothing else it's to protect the two of you."

I lean down and kiss her belly, and as she nods in agreement I kiss her, fiercely. I don't know if I am going to make it back but I don't want her to think that.

Grass pulls at my legs as I rush to the front door. It's standing ajar, moments ago I could feel the warmth of the sun beaming, but now I feel the icy chill that emanates from the house. I gulp and say a prayer as I push open the door. I fight the urge to turn back, I am terrified, but I have to be strong. For Kabrea, for Auntie, for my unborn child. I decide right then that if sacrificing myself is what it takes to save my loved one I am ready and willing. I step forward, ready to make a deal with the devil.

"Aunt T!" I yell, but nothing. I try again "Aunt T, where are you?!"

BOOM! The front door slammed behind me making me nearly jump out of my skin. So much for being brave, I think to myself. I look towards the kitchen, then down the hall, no sign of her anywhere. I head down the hallway, a hallway that once was filled with pictures of my family. The walls that held those pictures are now home to lots of mold, and cobwebs.

The first room on my left is my old room. I peak in, but am greeted by nothing but the smell of rotting wood.

"Auntie!" I call again, still no response. I begin to notice that the farther I walk down this hall, the colder it's getting. Shivering at this point, I walk to what was my mom and dad's room on my right. "Auntie, you in here?"

Not a sound, but as I stare into the darkroom, waiting for my eyes to adjust, I feel something; I Feel like someone is staring back at me. I back away, afraid to look away, then I take off as fast as I can into the last room. James' room. Trying to keep my steps light as the feeling of being watched grows stronger, I get to the doorway and I am about to call out to Tracie again when something grabs me by the arm and pulls me into the room.

I let out a small scream, and a hand immediately clamps over my mouth.

"Shhhh, boy." I hear,

whispered in my ear. My heart rate slows a bit as the familiar sound of Auntie's voice fills my head.

"Why are you here Kalen? Why would you come back here?"

I turn to face her. Body still trembling from the scare of being yanked in here.

"We were coming here today to finish this, and you called so we rushed here."

A bewildered look blankets her face, "Child.."

"Auntie she has to stop tormenting this family, and I'm ready to do whatever it takes to stop her."

"Stop talking like that Kalen, she will prey on your desperation, plus I've already offered myself son. I can't let her ruin anything else. I owe it to Keeshann to keep you all safe."

Tears rush down my face, she pulls me into a tight hug and I break. Suddenly we hear the whimpering outside the door. We look at each other and both drop to the floor.

"Kalen, promise me something."

"Anything."

"Please don't try to stop me. It will only make this harder than it is."

"No, please don't do this, we can find another way. I know we can." I beg.

"Now, you know that's not true; you walked up here with the same intentions. Except I beat you to it. And part of my deal is that I go willingly, as long as she lets you all alone. Let me save you, the way you saved me all these years." She says quietly as she cries silently.

We hear door after door slam, and we flinch after everyone. I am transported back to the night Mom and James were taken, laying here holding onto Auntie like this, it's happening all over again. BOOM! She's so close I can feel it in my bones, tears stream rapidly from my eyes as the door slowly opens. The woman stands in the doorway, featureless. Watching, waiting on what I am unsure.

"Thank you for allowing me to be your mom Kalen, I love you with all of my heart. You're going to be a great dad."

As the last words leave her lips she slips out of my arms and stands up.

"Take me, Take me and leave them alone!"

She looks back at me one last time, eyes glistening, making her hazel eyes shine.

"Please! No!" I manage between sobs as she is snatched from the room, door slamming behind her. "MOM!"

I stand frozen, afraid to move, to speak. I am that little boy again watching as another loved one is being taken away from me. "Fight, don't let her die," I tell myself. Crying memories flash in my mind about grandma, and grandpa, about mom and Auntie, the school kids who bullied me, and about James. I feel my fist tighten "fight Kalen push past this FIGHT!" Just then, I snap, all of my fear gone. I bolt out of the room following aunties screams, "MOM!"

I yelled as I raced down the hall. "Kalen, stay back," Auntie pleaded,

but I ignored her as I entered the dining room. Fear creeps up my spine once more, the woman's whimpering has ceased as she stands eye to eye with a now elevated Aunt Tracie. Before I could even think, I cried out,

"No, leave her alone,"

the woman's eyes shoot at me, dropping Aunt T to the floor. She glides slowly towards me, examining, her body moves gracefully, head shifting from side to side, but her eyes never leave mine.

"Stop Kalen right now!" Auntie yells, the woman doesn't flinch, and neither do I. I stood fixated on the woman wanting desperately to see her face. She's getting closer. Holding my breath for what comes next as I start to be lifted off the ground, "BOOM." Kabrea slams through the front door. The lady disappears,

CHAPTER 10

I fall hard to the floor. "Are you guys okay?" Kabrea says, rushing over to help.

"WHAT WERE YOU THINKING!? Auntie shouts at me with all her strength.

"I couldn't lose you too," I reply sadly. Aunty's face drops; tears leak from her eyes.

"We need to get rid of her once and for all," Kabrea says sternly and more aggressively than I've ever heard. Auntie and I nod our heads in agreement.

"But how?" Auntie chimes in,

having dealt with the woman her whole life.

"The Dr. Yes, Dr. Harris, he knows something!" I jump up, remembering one of our sessions. He knew something because of the way he froze up while I was talking.

"Dr. Harris?" Aunt T says

Kabrea, sharing in her confusion from the look on her face.

"Yes, during one of our sessions, I was telling him about my dream and the way he stopped talking and just glanced. He knows something we need to call him now." I say, hope in my voice, my phone already out of my pocket and into my hand. I don't care what time it is. He's told me on multiple different occasions that I can call him whenever I need him; Aunt T and Kabrea wait patiently as the phone begins to ring. "Pick up, please pick up," I plead after the second ring, the hope I was holding onto starts to drain. "Hello… Kalen," Dr. Harris answers,

I can tell I just woke him up. I don't say anything. I have so many questions, but I am drawing a blank

"Kalen, are you there? Is everything okay?"

Dr. Harris starts to get worried at my silence. Finally, I conjured up the courage to speak.

"Yes, I am here, but no, everything is not okay. I need you to tell me everything you know about the woman."

The line goes quiet. I'd think I was on mute if I didn't hear his deep breathing into the phone.

"This is very important. She is coming, Dr. Harris; she's coming for my family." I cry out, waiting for him to say anything. "Okay, Kalen, yes, I have had another case like this about ten years ago; my patient reported seeing the same woman in his dreams, and then she disappeared," he sniffled. He was crying.

"After she disappeared, I did a lot of research, hoping to find anything, and…" another pause; I got anxious, eager, and a little scared.

"She's called a Gello, or Gallû in Ancient Greek. She was said to threaten the reproductive cycle preying on their weak bodies and minds typically; she looks to possess her victims. But something has changed. This Gallû isn't looking to take control! She craves death and destruction. She corrupts the home of loving couples, causing them to fight; after that, a spontaneous fire kills a loved one forcing the others to seek some kind of explanation to find closure. The Gallû gets into people's heads talking to them, telling them how to see their loved ones again." Dr. Harris explains

I think about grandma and grampa and how Auntie told me they were so in love, then mom and dad hearing all this, I place the phone on speaker so that Auntie and Kabrea can also listen as the doctor keeps talking about the woman.

"As she inserts herself into a family home, there is little you can do to get rid of her. She pretends to be who you believe you've lost, tricking you into acceptance."

Aunt T's eyes grow wide like she's realized something, but she doesn't say anything.

"In ancient times, people used charms, magical stones, and amulets which then turned to crosses and holy water as Christianity grew, but these are short term effects."

"How do we get rid of her for good!?" Kabrea shouts with anger. Auntie and I stand puzzled at the sudden outburst, but we share her frustration, and we await an answer from Dr. Harris, but there is silence, my heart racing. She's gone right now. She will return, and we don't know when or where. "Dr. Harris, we need to know how to get rid of this Gallû, please if you know."

Before Aunt T could finish her sentence, Dr. Harris cuts her off.

"I don't know. I wish I did, but I don't know."

I can tell he is crying if he knew more; he would definitely tell us the phone now, just sniffles and heavy breathing. "Thank you, doctor, really, thank you so much," I finally say, breaking the awkwardness between us all.

"If I could do more, I would, Kalen, keep your family safe; please call me back if you need anything. Goodnight."

"Goodnight," I reply,

knowing no one will get a wink of sleep tonight. I think back to when the doctor lied to me, knowing the woman was out there. Still, he said I imagined the woman that me and Aunt T conjured the woman up in our minds, and he knew the whole time I get frustrated but quickly let it go, Dr. Harris was just trying to protect me maybe or he just didn't want to believe it was happening again which I understand.

"I am scared," I finally admitted to everyone, including myself we stayed silent, huddled as close as possible till the sun began to rise over the trees, street lights started to wither away. I begin to think about James, his nappy black hair that he loved to call curly. He was so tall to me back then but was only 5'8. He always used to tell me I would never be taller than him, but I'm 5'10, so I win; I guess James was a class clown but was also top in his class in academics. He played two varsity sports and always made it home on time to help mom with dinner. I remember crying one night, and he came into my room and sat on the floor beside me till I could fall asleep. His girlfriend or, as he would say, his high school sweetheart. I can't recall her name though I really wish he was here now. James always knew what to do or what to say. I wish he could have met Kabrea. They would have loved each other.

"I love you."

I say to Kabrea, admiring her glow, her soft hands holding tightly on mine, the sun starting to shine in, putting a slight glare on her glasses, making it impossible to see her green eyes, brown hair pulled into a messy bun to keep out of her face she doesn't move, but she speaks

"I love you too."

She says softly

"Kalen, we have to do something; we have to get rid of the woman,"

Kabrea says more intensely than I expected

"She's right, Kalen."

Aunt T finally speaking up, her lips still quivering;

"How," I protest, "how can we stop it, her, the damn demon."

I say with fear, anger, and exhaustion in my voice Kabrea sits still; I can tell she's thinking of a plan. She has a look of determination on her face. Auntie gets up heading towards the room that was her dad's office

"If there's a way to summon her, there has to be a way to get rid of her," Aunt T says, walking angrily

"Auntie, there's nothing in there; if we wanna do research, let's go to the library or search our phones. I mean, they have google."

I jokingly say, trying to lighten the mood, and it worked as Kabrea and Aunt T let out a little chuckle.

"We can do both; check the internet at the library; let's go."

Aunt T says she was always good at dividing and conquering. We rush out of the house, not worrying at all about cosmetics. Aunt T insists on driving. She hates being in the car with me going anywhere and says I am reckless, which is ridiculous if you ask me, but she and Kabrea agree, so I don't argue. We get to the library as the librarian is unlocking the doors to open, and she must have seen the distress on our faces because she didn't ask any questions at all. She just opened the door for us to come on in

"Books on voodoo, supernatural, or demons where would they be"

The lady's eyes widen a couple of inches as she scans all of us before speaking

"Section 12 books about religion"

She points in the direction we need to go; still a little shocked at our inquiry, we move past her swiftly and quietly. I plop at the table next to our section and grab my phone out to browse the web for answers. Aunt T and Kabrea start to rifle through the publications for anything that we could use, grabbing books on voodoo, black magic, the truth about demons; my body shakes as I find names like Lilith, Gallû, and Abezu

"Demons weaken knowing their names," I say excitedly, having gotten some information

"Shhhh," the librarian shoots me a dirty glimpse with her finger pressed on her lips tightly

"Sorry," I say softly with my most innocent look. Aunt T and Kabrea have made it to the table with a couple of books each and started to rummage through them, both fast readers who aren't easily distracted as they read. I notice the lights flicker, and I freeze. My heart starts to skip, and my hands get sweaty, but Aunt T and Kabrea still sit unfazed, so I slowly begin to calm down

"YOUR MINE!" the woman said, the lights completely shut off; I jump up, pushing my chair behind me with a hard knock on the hardwood floor

"Shhhh, please, or you'll have to leave," the librarian says, annoyed

"Are you okay? What happened" Kabrea whispered to me, still standing, goosebumps creeping up and around my body

"She's here; we need to hurry," I managed to say before… Everything went black.

"Kalen, wake up, sweety."

That voice is so familiar, warm, so loving.

"Kalen, come on time to get up."

I sit up slowly; what is happening? I am in my childhood bed. The red power ranger stares back at me as I pull my head from my pillow sunlight floods the room

"Good morning"

I turn to face the mystery voice

"MOM!"

I holler as my voice gets shaky. My eyes start to water, and my body feels fragile.

"What's going on?"

I say, Confused, my emotions running rampant.

"Come on, you're always such a goofball in the morning, Kalen. It's time to get ready for school."

Keeshann says, pulling me up from my bed, and before she can turn to walk out, I grab and hug her tightly

"I love you, mom."

I cry onto her shoulder, not wanting ever to let her go again

"I love you too, buddy," Keeshann says, squeezing me in her arms

"Now, get ready for school," she demands, exiting the room; I follow her, not knowing what else to do. As I leave the room, I end up at the dinner table with my mom and James. They begin to talk about their day. More specifically, James talks about sports while mom pretends to know what he is talking about our typical dinner. I fight the urge to jump out of my chair and embrace James. I fight the urge to cry; instead, I sit and enjoy whatever this is. I let out a sigh, and a big smile creeps across my face; the room goes pitch black. I can't see a thing as my eyes start to focus again. I am back in my room. It's dark out, and an eerie sensation tingles through the air

"No, you can't have him!" mom sternly says

"you promised him to me he's mine," a menacing voice replies

I jumped up out of my bed, terrified. My first instinct is to hide to stay completely quiet,

"No, I won't let you take him away from me; I won't let you kill my son." mom says, standing her ground

"Then I will take you both," the demonic voice growls. I hear a scuffle, and before I could move to see what was happening, mom burst through my room door, pulling me from my bed and racing out as fast as she entered. We run into James's room, who is already on his feet

"Keep him safe, close the door, and don't leave this room," mom demands

"But mom," James protest

"NO James, I mean it." mom yells back

Darkest Nights

James stands frozen, tears pooling in his eyes. He wants to stay strong, but he's about to break. Mom kisses us both on the forehead. "I love you both so much,"

she says as she closes the door slowly.

"Kalen, Kalen, wake up."

I wake to see Kabrea and Aunt T standing over me.

"What happened," I ask

"You jumped up out of your chair afraid; then you passed out. We were seconds away from calling 911." Aunt T explains

"I saw mom and James." my voice catches as I hold back tears. Aunt T and Kabrea look shocked at first before Kabrea turns and grabs a book

"We found something," Kabrea says, flipping open a book on demonology

"The reason she stopped after she killed your grandfather is that he offered himself to her," she says, pausing and looking at me for a second like she is gathering the strength to proceed

"Your mom conjured her back up, which started the cycle over again." Kabrea continues

"But she took my mom; she took James," I say, finally letting myself cry, but as I say it, I remember my dream from a moment ago mom rejected the woman, so she took both her and James

"It wasn't an offering; mom tried to fight the woman, and she killed them both," I explain to Kabrea and Aunt T; trying to gauge their reaction Kabrea sits beside me with the book in her hands and points at a paragraph

"This is how we get rid of her for good."

To get her out of our lives for good, we have to destroy her place of origin. or the place she was summoned

"The place she was summoned so the old house," I say a little too loud as the librarian stares holes into my soul

CHAPTER 11

"Yes, we have to destroy your old house to be rid of the woman," Kabrea says,

Letting out a breath as if she was holding it this whole time, we all sat in silence for a couple of seconds before getting up. Auntie gives instructions on how we are going to get the job executed. My head is in shambles; I can't think straight. Will this really be over? The woman has been a constant in my life for so long tears of joy of hope start to gloss my eyes

"So we will go to the house tonight so no one will see us. We will douse it in gasoline and burn it down for good this time." Aunt T says

Determination in her eyes, a hint of anger as well; after all, Aunt T has been dealing with the woman much longer than I have. "This will be one of the darkest nights of our lives." Aunt T says

"And the latest longest," I add

I see the house in the distance. As we get closer, I feel my body tense up as Kabrea grabs my hand

"We can do this. Let's kill this bitch" Kabrea says, Smirking

"And be done with her for good," Aunt T says strongly

As we pull into the driveway, the darkness of the night surrounds us. My heart pounds with anticipation with fear. As we slowly exit the car, the wind whispers through the surrounding houses. The creatures of the night seem to hide, sensing their own mortality. Tallgrass brushing against my legs, weeds growing on and around the porch, the front door lies slightly open, as leaves blow in and out, making the house look as if it's breathing, my heart beating so loudly I wonder if Aunt T or Kabrea could hear, but I charge forward

"Ready?" Aunt T asked

Her face shows nothing but strength, eye narrow and jaw clenching

"Ready as we will ever get," I admit

A little less hopeful than Auntie, we step into the house and immediately head to the end of the hall, start from the back and work our way forward. "BOOM, CLICK " the door slams behind us and locks, but we don't waver, rushing to the end of the hall with our gallon of gasoline. The light from the moon slowly fades as if a blanket is being tossed over the top

"We have to hurry," Kabrea whispers

Fear that the Woman might be listening, Kabrea and Aunt T pull out their flashlight as I start to pour the gas dumping it angrily on every surface I can see

"YOUR MINE" a demonic roar brings all of us to a complete stop, then we hear the whimpering followed by the footsteps

"What do we do?" I cry, now panicking

"Let's get this done, Kalen. Come on," Aunt T says aggressively and looks at me with all the courage she can muster

I nod. We race out of one room to the next, scattering gas all over the house. The woman's whimpering gets louder the closer we get to the front of the house. As we walk into the kitchen, the flashlights start to flicker, but we dismiss it and move on before realizing we are in complete darkness. The dining room was cold enough to see the smoke from our breath. We huddle close together. The house seems to be closing in around us as the woman begins to apparate on the other side of the room. "RUN" Kabrea shouts, grabbing my hand to run towards the front door; Aunt T follows close behind. We scramble to get the door open, but it won't budge

"AHHHHH," Aunt T screams

We turn, the woman is face to face with Aunt T

"The child belongs to me." the woman seethed

"You will not touch my child!." I shout

My rage overpowering my fear

"Then I will take you all." Gallû insist

Aunt T beings to lift, but I reach my hand up and grab hers, holding on tightly Kabrea pounds at the door with all her might,

"BANG, BANG, CRACK, the door gives way

I pull Aunt T as hard as I can. The woman's grip reduces, forcing us into the front door, breaking it open. We all fall out onto the porch. Aunt T is on her feet immediately. She pulls the matches from her pocket

"Die, you bitch!" Aunt T yells, swiping the match and throwing it into the house

"RUN," Kabrea shouts

The House is engulfed in flames in seconds as we run to the car and drive off without even a glance back; the tension is gone, a smile creeps onto Kabrea's face as she lays her head on my shoulder, we remain quiet but we can hear sirens in the distance

"Aunt T, can we stay with you tonight" I plead

"Yes, of course, Kalen," Aunt says, her voice falling short from exhaustion

I can tell she's tired. We all are. We pull into Aunt T's ready for bed Kabrea struggling to keep her eyes open Aunt T refuses to go to sleep before she showers and watches the news i plop down onto the couch before I can grab the remote Auntie snatches it and turns on Channel 12 headline reads mysterious fire in suburbs....

House still intact

www.ingramcontent.com/pod-product-compliance
Lightning Source LLC
LaVergne TN
LVHW020433080526
838202LV00055B/5171